Why Should Boys have all the pain?

Flairs and Glairs

Publication House

"Why should boys have all the pain?"

ISBN No: " 978-93-90416-82-0"
1st Edition
Language – English and Hindi

Flairs and Glairs
Publication House
Regd. Under MSME Act.

Copyright. 2020, Muskan Shah

Disclaimer

This is a work of fiction and solely represent the thoughts of the corresponding authors of the articles. Our editors have tried their best to edit the content of all the authors and check the plagiarism.

All the write-ups in this book are unique and are only published in this book.

In case any plagiarism or error is found, only the author is responsible alone, and not the publisher or the Compilers.

Cover Designing
Shubham Shah

Acknowledgement

My primary thanks to God. I am blessed with the energy to be able to complete this anthology.
I am also thankful towards our whole team of "Flairs and Glairs Publication".

I am thankful to my parents, Mr. Ashok Shah and Mrs. Archana Shah for trusting and supporting me always. And my friends and extended family to support in every step of life. And to provide me a surrounding where I can raise my voice for all types of issues.

Thankyou, all the co-authors, without your support we would never be able to complete this anthology

Introduction

Boys, best part of every life and yet ignored, pressured, and judged. Why do they face discrimination starting from childhood??

"BOYS DON'T CRY" we don't understand who made this rule, boys are stronger both physically and mentally, agreed, but they are humans too, they deserve equal treatment as well.

Boys don't show but they feel, understand its important.

Boys are beautiful creatures, understand and value them.

Because, *"Why should boys have all the pain??"*

Co Authors

1. Shubham Shah (Founder Flairs and Glairs
2. Ishani Agarwal (Co Founder Flairs and Glairs))
3. Muskan Shah (Compiler)
4. Abhigna Mudogonda
5. Abhilash Rout
6. Abhiram B.
7. Akanksha Sakhuja
8. Aditya
9. Aishwarya V.J.
10. Aman Kumar
11. Arya Ojha
12. Asfia Hayat Khanam
13. Asraya
14. Chahat Kanchan
15. Christy Gnana Deepa. J
16. Deepak Babu
17. Deepanshu Singhal
18. Deepjyoti Chowdhury
19. Gaurangi Singh
20. Hansika SR
21. Harshavardini.M
22. Ishani Durba Purkayastha
23. Jeevitha S.
24. J. Josephine Jesika
25. Jyoti Matania
26. Madhu Singh
27. Mansha Poddar
28. Meghana Dumpala

29. Meghna Chatterjee
30. Muskan Sachdeva
31. Nanci Kabra
32. Nithya Kanagaraj
33. Pinki Bansal
34. Prachi Shah
35. Priyanka Varma
36. Priyanshu Somkuwar
37. Rahul Sain
38. Rahul Raj Srivastava
39. R. Susanna Celsia
40. Sahina Ghugha
41. Samikhya Swain (Ikhya)
42. Sapna Bhatt
43. Shikhar Pathak
44. Shivani Sarwade
45. Sheela Suman
46. Shreya Gupta
47. Sonal Tripathi Mishra
48. Subananthini. R
49. Suhita S.
50. Surbhi Bairagi
51. V. Heymonth Kumar
52. Yamini Sona Vaishnavi
53. Yumkham Shelina Devi

Shubham Shah

(Founder- Flairs and Glairs)

Shubham Shah, entrepreneur at "Flairs & Glairs" a brand with dynamics in events organizing and cultural educational pan INDIA, He is a 26yr. old guy who recently has entered, the digital platform of imprinting emotions. He has initiated with his own open mic platform to help budding poets and aspiring writers under his brand named as "Teekhe Zasbaaat"

He is a commerce graduate from Bhagalpur City of Bihar.

He says Writing has impersonated him since childhood and he has now been writing for over a decade!

Cooking, on the other hand, is his passion! He also mentions, trying out new things just tickles him!

When asked sir, Why SPICY EMOTIONS?

He smiled and added, "agar jasbaat teekhe na ho toh wo jasbaat kaha" Spices are all that blends! So do his words!
As a chef, he presents to you his dish! Hot and freshly served! Taste it! Feel it! Enjoy it! You can also find his writing in the Solo book "Teekhe Zasbaaat" and 70+ anthologies. With his passion to explore opportunities across Platforms he is working with keen devotion and We wish him all the very best for his future ventures
Share your reviews on his

INSTAGRAM

@spicy_emotions
@shubham4shah

Or via email on

shubham2shah@gmail.com

To stay tuned to his work and opportunities follow his business Handles

INSTAGRAM   FACEBOOK   YOUTUBE

@flairsandglairs
@teekhezasbaaat

WEBSITE:

https://flairsandglairs.in/
https://flairsandglairs.com/

Ishani Agarwal

(Co Founder- Flairs and Glairs)

Ishani Agarwal
Born and brought up in Kolkata, she has done her schooling and college from here itself. She is doing her post-graduation at the moment. Ishani loves talking to people around, and is excited for this new beginning of hers! Been a Compiler for 35+ Anthologies, and in the process for more, also, co-authored in 100+ Anthologies, Ishani is very Happy with how her life is turning out now!
Insta handle: Ishani_agarwal_quotes

Compiler
Muskan Shah

'I follow dreams to make them reality'
Muskan Shah, a girl from Jharsuguda, Odisha. Currently a Company Secretary Professional Student, followed her dreams of an Interior Designer.
A writer and a Poetess. Being a writer, she writes all genre: stories, articles, quotes, content's, etc. And being a poetess, she writes poetries and Poems are her forte. She has a dream to be

known as a Poet in the world for her poetries and beautiful pieces.

She not dreams of being a writer but also working hard to fulfill the same. Her journey till date has been amazing by being a compiler of 6 Anthologies and a co-author of 50+ Anthologies.

Instagram Handle – The_Unpublished.Ink

क्या लड़के इंसान नहीं है?

कर उम्मीद लड़को से सारी
तुम उनको ही सुनाते हो
लड़के काबिल होते है, कहते हो
फिर उन्हें है नीचा दिखाते हो

कुछ झूठी लड़कियों के आंसुओं पे तुम
पूरा देश लुटाते हो
और लड़के की बातें बयान बता कर
बिन जुर्म की सज़ा उनसे कटवाते हो

रोते नहीं है लड़के
ये बचपन से सिखाते हो
लड़के भी इंसान होते है
ये क्यों नहीं बताते हो

बोझ उठाओ सारे, काम है तुम्हारा
ये हर बात पे उसे बताते हो
हाथो में चूड़ियां पहन लो घर पे रहना है अगर
वो कुछ मां का हाथ बटा दे तो भी, उसे ही सुनाते हो

सब्र करें वो इंसान भी कब तक
तुम इतना उसे सताते हो
वाह रे दुनिया तरीके तेरे
लड़को को जरूरत बोल, तुम लड़को को ही बेगैरत बताते हो

लड़कियों पे जुर्म कुछ कम नहीं है
इस बात से दुनिया वाकिफ है
पर लड़को की भी ज़िन्दगी आसान नहीं है
ये क्यों नहीं किसी को समझाते हो

पैसे कमाने से लेकर घर चलाने तक
सारी उम्मीदें तुम लड़कों से लगाते हो
जो चूक गए अगर कुछ कही वो
तो सारा दोष उन्हीं पे गड़ जाते हो

लड़कों को समझो इंसान है वो भी
ये क्यों नहीं दुनिया को बताते हो
लड़के दर्द क्यों सहे सारा
ये नारा क्यों नहीं लगाते हो?

समझो अब जरूरी है
एक और मानव सिंह के मरने का इंतज़ार मत करो
लड़को हमेशा गलत नहीं होते
उन्हें समझो और इंसानों सा बर्ताव करो।।

Ishika Agarwal

Ishika is a 16 years old girl.

Writing for her is nothing else but a passion. She hails from the city of Joy and Art. She has been a Co-author in 30+ anthologies in the recent past, all adding on experiences to her.

Been a part of India book of Record projects like Black and World Record projects like 15 wonders of Poetry, Ishika is paving her way to success.

(1)

Why should boys have all the privileges?
Why should they have all the rights?
Why should girls be in control rather than boys?
My main question is WHY. I am a girl but I want to live my life like every boy can live.
I wanna go on solo trips.
I wanna go clubbing.
I wanna party.
I wanna ride a bike.
But everyone asks me "what will people say?"
I say I don't are.
I wanna live my life like anybody else and I will live my life my way!

Abhigna Mudigonda

She is Abhigna Mudigonda from Andhra Pradesh(vijayawada). Currently, she is pursuing her B-tech in EEE from VR Siddhartha Engineering college, Vijayawada. She is the innovative club coordinator and Project club head volunteer from EEE department in VR Siddhartha engineering college. Apart from these, she loves writing as she writes what she feels and hope that you like the work contributed by her here.

<u>I wish, I should have lived in my mother's womb!!!</u>

He should have lived in his mother's womb,
rather than being born as a conqueror,
in this societal posture of an ideal men.

Being portrayed as a strong man,
he closed the door to let out his vulnerabilities.
So, sometimes he felt those deep-down emotions,
and sometimes he didn't.
In a weird battle, struggling to maintain,
that constant balance of love and partnership of life.

Tears held inside,
hidden deep down.
Craving for that softer shadow of himself,
to be represented out before this world.
But he shut down to live as a responsible person,
in the process of taking care of his family's burdens.
And lost the touch of love, pain and sadness.

Finally, in the olden days of life's path
when he has seen his loved one's death.
He didn't know how to react.
On the inside, he is dying, screaming for her touch,
But on the outside, he chose to remain silent.
And forget all the pain before someone catches it.

Finally, in his last stages,
Sleeping on his bed from a side, he told to himself,
I should have lived in my mother's womb,
rather than being born as a conqueror,
in this societal posture of an ideal man.

Abhilash Rout

Abhilash Rout is from Cuttack, Odisha. He has completed his graduation in B.Com with Accounts Honors. He is preparing for competitive exams too. He has been working for the welfare of working out for the weaker sections of the society. Writing has been a part of expressing his feelings & his thoughts into words. He is working in Odia film industry as an actor, story writer and assistant director. His Instagram handle is @coolcapt_abhilash. He has taken part in more than 145 anthologies which includes international anthologies too.

Boy are not always wrong

We live in a very complicated society,
where it is very difficult for a boy to
live a normal life,
as with the advancement of time
and rules have changed like anything.
People start blaming the boy prior to a girl,
but many a times it is just the opposite
way around.
Sometimes the girl may also be wrong
or she may have used her powers in a
negative way which really have a wrong
impact on the society.
But sometimes we forget that our father,
brother are also boys,
they too have a heart and they too have
want respect, love attention too.
We should see that everyone should be
treated equally.

Boys Do Have A Heart

We all have come across such situations
in our life where boys really feel depressed,
as they do a lot of works but they didn't get
appreciations but instead they are tortured
in the name of a husband, a son, a father etc.
Boys too have a heart like all they too need
special attentions and special caring,
but the corrupted society have forced them
to wear a fake mask of manhood.
Boys have got to play the role of a son, a
husband and a father where he is divided in
such a way that they get stuck in them.
When a boy gets married then it becomes his
responsibilities to take care of his parents,
his in-laws and his wife too,
but in maximum cases what happens is that
sometimes if he gets busy in looking after
one person then the second person too start
complaining about their characters.
All boys are stuck in similar situations,
but they are ready to so but they too want
some special treatments and special affection from their
loved ones too.

Abhiram B.

Hailing from Alleppey, Kerala; and a medical student in GMC (RIMS), Ongole, Andhra Pradesh, he is a technology freak, and likes reading, writing, travelling, listening to songs and watching movies. He likes writing whatever it comes to his mind, and likes writing poems, stories, micro tales and motivational quotes.

<u>A Boy isn't Everyone's Wallet</u>

Always I am irritated
By everyone for me buying things
Even for smallest things
They would ask me,
And that too
Without giving me back the money
That they spent from mine!

I would too be frustrated
Like anyone
When they also become
In a situation like that,
But I do stand my cool
So that I won't cause any trouble
For anyone.

But that has become too much
For me,
And I couldn't tolerate whatever
They started asking to me
To spend on whatever, they want.
I would tell that
Those people are poor or what,
Just begging from us
For no reason, and spending for
Things which they wanted the most

Why nowadays people
Wanted to ask from us?

They can hard work
And get some money from anywhere, right?

These questions are the ones
Which every boy must ask
To everyone,
Because, we boys also are hardworking
For some living,
And that requires money.

Money isn't the one
Which falls from a tree,
Rather, it is dig from the sand
By our hard work.

Akanksha Sakhuja

Akanksha Sakhuja, from Jamshedpur, is a proud alumuni of D.B.M.S School. She has presently completed her Graduation in English Honors with flying colors. Her writing gives a way out to her deep and intense passion for literature. She is looking forward to pursue her masters to enhance her qualification. Akanksha is keen on writing good quotes and short stories. Being a good orator she has been an active participant in literary activities in school and at college like debate and speeches etc. Akanksha has a keen interest in reading and to pen down her own experiences which is her uniqueness. She looks forward to teaching and writing as a career. It is just a beginning a long way to go new challenges to overcome.

Pillar of our life

Everybody faces some or other difficulties in their lives, but we are supported by some special bond of Men around us. We always regard men as the strongest and dominating part of our society. And we have a preconception that it's their responsibility to support as a well as protect the women of our society, it's their responsibility to earn, or their duty to take care of their family only. But sometimes their protection turns to possessiveness, which is not likeable, and we regard them as wrong.

But they aren't!
I have faced one of such experience in my life where I supported some inaccurate act which was aborning in my friend's life. She was in a relationship for two years and used to boost a lot. among our friend group. Everybody used to flatter her even I was one among them. But suddenly, her nature her dressing as well as her interest started to shift to another guy which was very un-usual, so as her friend I enquired about the matter, she with full of pain and with a heavy hard she shared the matter to me , Abhishek, her ex-boyfriend blackmailed her and mentally harassed her . Hearing this made my blood boil, and I wanted my friend should get justice and nobody should blame her for the end of the relationship

I started being friendly with Abhishek and poked as much as possible into the matter, but I was stunned to know the truth, that it was Priya (my friend) who was the guilty one and not Abhishek, he showed me all the chats between them and it was she who ditched Abhishek because he was not able to fulfill her demands. I realized my mistake that without knowing the truth I directly jumped to conclusion, and I always had a notion that boys in the relationship are the most corrupt one and girls are innocent. But to my utter surprise, Priya turned to be untrustworthy.

And, since that day I have stopped judging the "Men" of our society, and they are not to be blamed for every mistake. I totally agree they are always not wrong. And I want my society should also accept this truth.

Aditya

Aditya is from Amethi; Uttar Pradesh. He had opened his door to this world on 21 October ;2005
He is Cadet of Sainik School Gopalganj
He loves writing articles and reading novels.

The Blind Believe

Girl are the goddess of this world. They are the one who continue our generation. They are the one who always serve in better way.   We should respect them. We should have faith in them. We should care about them. But; we should remember that there are boys also in this world. We should have faith in them but we should remember that our faith and trust should not get blindly. We can take example from our daily life "We have sister in our house and we observe that the love and kind of affection which our sister get from our relatives and parents is totally different than that of her brother. She will get more love and affection than her brother. And this not only remain in house. We could have more examples like that such as " If a boy hand get touched to the body of a girl by mistake then that girl without knowing that she had been touched accidentally she just overreact and tell everybody that the boy was intensely touching her and her parent also without listening to the verdict of boy they directly blame the boy .

Taking advantage of this blindly faith girls do various crime they make boys behind bars without any reason by just saying that the boy was molesting her. And the question which arises after all this is that. Why, always boys have pain? And this question should arise. We should think that always boys are not wrong. We should think that always the verdict of girls is not the true sometimes verdict of boys also gets true. We should believe in girls but not blindly. We should change our mind regarding boys. We should not always blame on boys because sometimes "_Papa ki pari_ also do mistakes. And When this will be the thinking of everyone in this world then the question. Why boys always have pain??? Stop!!!

Aishwarya VJ

Aishwarya, hails from Coimbatore, Tamil Nadu. She completed her schooling from Keartiman Academy. Currently, she is pursuing her bachelorette of commerce. Writing was not a profession but somehow became passion for her. She is a budding writer and a published co-author. She is in part of many anthologies. Instagram handle - @aishubieber.

Why?

"Can I hang out?" He asked,
"be a responsible man", said his family.
"You are thin!
gain some weight man", said his fellow mates.
"What is your income?
Will you be able to look after your family?", asked many.
"You are infertile!
Are you even man?", many laughed.
"Don't cry like a lady!
being a man, you should not cry", said the society.
"Can I kiss my teen daughter?", he asked,
"No, you are not allowed", said the society.
"Don't be funny!
behave like a gentleman", said everyone.
"Why?", He asked,
"because you are a man", said the world.

Aman Kumar

अमन कुमार एक सरल विचार और साधारण व्यक्ति हैं| इनका जन्म बिहार के पटना जीला में सन् 7 जुलाई 1998 को हुआ था| ये अभी इंजीनियरिंग से डिप्लोमा कर रहे हैं| ये अभी 10+ anthologies में सह लेखक हैं और इन्हें शायरी,कहानी और गाने लिखने का भी शौक है|

हम ही क्यों

हम ही क्यों,
क्योंकि हम लड़के हैं,
जीवन के बोझ हम ढ़ोएं,
हर किसी के ताने हम सुने,
जन्म होते जिम्मेदारीयों को हम याद रखें,
किसी के गलती की डांट भी हम सुने,
हम ही क्यों,
क्योंकि हम लड़के हैं|

हमारा दिल जैसे मोम नहीं कोई पत्थर का हो,
दिल टूटने पर गम में हम डूब जाएं,
हर टूटे रिश्ते की वजह हम हो जाएं,
गम ना जताएं तो बेवफा हम कहलाएं,
हम ही क्यों,
क्योंकि हम लड़के हैं|

बेवजह ही खुद को पत्थर-सा सख्त हो जाएं,
आखों से बहते आंसू के हर बुंद पी जाएं,
दिल में उठते दर्द को हम किसी कोने में दफन कर जाएं,
हर दफा गलती हमारी हो ये वाजिब तो ना हो जाएं,
हम ही क्यों,
क्योंकि हम लड़के हैं|

Arya Ojha

Arya ojha is a poetess.

She loves to write and recite poetry. Anchoring, Crafting are other combination of her hobbies. She had participated in various anthologies which is going to be released soon. Her Instagram handle is @unplugged.soul where she has wonderful piece of write-ups.

<u>Boys – Their tangled life</u>

A boy with smile,
Thousand miles.
The pain he suffers,
No one measures.

The responsibility he owes,
No one really knows,
Everyone just asked,
Burdens are masked.

As soon as he grows,
The manliness rows,
Family teaches the same,
Boys who cry are lame.

The earning pressure,
The responsibility fresher,
The characters validity,
As they are for pity.

The fake feminism,
Shadows from a prism,
Boys also need to be heard,
Like a flying bird.

Not all the boys are same,
Proving them is your aim,
Coins have two-sided face,
Judge after proving a race.

Asfia hayat khanam

Asfia hayat khanam, from West Bengal, 20 years old, undergraduate student of Aligarh Muslim University, she is very much passionate about writing, she wants to change the views, perspectives, mentality and life of people from her writing.

She wants to fight for women's and girl's empowerment, independence, rights and want to be the voice of all the needy persons.

She wants to end the concept of gender discrimination, fake feminism, patriarchal system from our society.

<u>Different roles of boys</u>

Why we forget that the same boy plays the role of father in our life where he provides us all the facilities to live a beautiful life, give us everything, give freedom for education, provide us happiness, without thinking about himself.

The same boy plays the role of brothers, who protect us from all the other bad boys, stood beside us in every difficult situation and support us.

The same boy plays the role of best friend who accompany us in everything, never take us in wrong way, never have bad intentions for us and never misuse us.

The same boy plays the role of life partner who understands us, respect us, give us a happy life, don't put restriction on us, allow us to live our life according to our own terms.

The same boy play the role of a son where he shows the society what her mother teaches him the good things and how he is different from other bad boys.

And there are some stranger boys also who protect us from other boys' evil eyes in different situations and respect us.

Not every boy is wrong

When something bad happens to any girl and she put allegations on boy then why we without knowing the actual truth we just start blaming the boy that yes he is wrong it's not necessary that every time the boys are wrong and girls are correct, our constitution has make laws to arrest the criminals but we people before considered that person as a criminal before proving their crimes.

There might be something else happen may be the girl was lying, playing girl card and fake feminism.
Don't boys get hurt, don't they cry, don't they feel weak: they do feel all the things which a girl feel or which a normal human being should feel, they are not robots or made up of steels but this society has just framed a different image of boys in front of every that boys should be hard, strong with a macho man figure and because of this boys always has to put a fake image of their selves in -front of everyone.
There are many boys who end up their life due to the fake allegation they do have their self-respect and they are also concerned about their self-respect.
Society has given girls the title of fake feminism and they can do anything in this title they can abuse boys, harasses them, cheat them, use them but boys can't do this same and then we talk about equality, if we need equality then it should be in every platform.

Asraya. Raj

Asraya is a final year BSc. nursing student. She is from Kerala. Apart from studies her passion is writing. She became co-author in the Flashed rhythm anthology by flair and glair publications. This is her 2nd writings that has been published. And, she is so glad to be a part of this book.

<u>Not every boy is Devil</u>

My soul speaks to you,
You might have been abused in the dew.
I accept only the 'real one' inside you.
Scratch in you doesn't mean the ruin.
There are many, who plays just for the name.
Powerful man is those - who come in-front.
My love for you is not a lust.
In fact, it's not a desire, not a seduce
and something so...
It's nothing but - you are part of my better half.
Can't replace with any of the feeling of behalf.
However, the good man can only be, with your soul....and not
with your body.
So that, every girl should realize that not every boy is devil.
There are some, who really touches the innate essence of a
girl.

Let love for all, be a rule

Domain of oneself is not the need. Instead we want equality for both genders. Feminism and meninism is the thing to tear and scatter. Man, in the darkness may be a vulture. But don't see all as the same. It's just the thought of our society...to seal everyone in their black. There exists man with good principles. They are the real heroes, capable of taking care of their loved ones, even in their difficulties. Helps them to embrace their darkness. And teach them to dance in the rain of opportunities. Actually, life has no rules, man make it and implement it. That leads to violence and corruptions and at last that's the base of developing ego between men and women. Boys can't be the master of all crimes. Whereas, they face that label. They also get suffered, depressed, abused and getting exploited.

Boys also deserve some rights. But no one seems to come forward for their rights. It's the time to accept them. They are too, humans. They too have emotions, pains and feelings. Don't keep them aside. Help each other and just move on.

Chahat Kanchan

Herself Chahat kanchan. She is just trying to complete her mother desire. If you think "Chahat" is her name, so What do you mean by "Kanchan". Actually, she uses her mother name as her last name. She has only one dream and aim that "Her name may vanish away from world, but her mother name will stay forever & ever in people heart". She started her writing when she was just in 8 class, but gives her way of writing to explore and express herself after she completed her secondary school. Her writing dream is she wants to inspire more and more people through her ink. She has only temptation for LOVE & BLESSINGS and wants THANK TO GOD. She loves to being Introvert and want to remains a mystery...!!
Insta - @KanchanChahat

<u>He - Heals Me.</u>

Why should he??
Can't be free
The load of work
The headache of me

Pay the money,
I want this HONEY!!
Oh, I am sad!!
Do role of funny,

He just allow,
The expensive gift for her WAOOW!!
He is always there,
When a girl's say " NOW "

The pressure of family,
The job of stress,
How much he did for you,
Girls say "LESS"

The effort of loyal boy,
You can't explain,
Just for few Jerk girl,
All girl suffers the pain.

It's not gender,
About man to women,
Understand everyone

Do for them whatever you can!

He is not always wrong,
Some be YOUR DOVE
Some only say few words,
Some boys prove their "LOVE"!!

Christy Gnana Deepa. J

Christy Gnana Deepa , compiler, writer pursuing her Under graduate in English literature in Madurai, Tamil Nadu, India. She is also a compiler of an anthology SECLUDED HEARTS. she is a co-author of more than 10 Anthologies. A writer by passion and a literarian by profession. She is a Wattpad writer too. Check her out in Instagram as ___budding___writer

<u>The Vim Powerhouse</u>

He is the high caliber of life,
Also, he reconciles every strife,
He is not always wrong,
But, never forgets to stay strong.

He does things anonymous,
With great magnanimous.
He holds great company always
And his influence sways.

He, the safeguard and defender,
The great benefactor and sympathizer,
With him, I am ultrasafe,
And never lets me unsafe.

He does everything for me,
And he is my honey bee.
Even in troubles, he never leaves
But together grieves.

He is together strong;
Happy as the day is long;
He is not always wrong
Even saves us from the throng.

Deepak Babu

यह दीपक प्रधान जी हैं पिता श्री जगदीश प्रधान, इन्हें हर कोई प्यार से दीपक बाबू भी कहता है।बचपन से माँ का साया उठने के बाद बहुत टूट से गए थे,हालात ओर बेबसी ने लिखना सीखा दिया

सुरु से किताब लिखने की ललक ने शायर गजलकार बना दिया ओर देखते-देखते अपनी स्वलिखित दो डायरिया लिख दी।

दीप बाबू मध्य प्रदेश के धार जिले के धामनोद नामक नगर में निवास करते हैं, यह वर्तमान में धार जिले के मनावर नगर में बैंक सहायक कर्मचारी के पद पर कार्यरत है। यह ग्रेजुवेट हे,इनकी प्रारंभिक शिक्षा सरकारी स्कूल से ही सम्प्पन हुई है।स्कूल समय से लेखन दुनिया में अपना लोहा मनवा चुके,तब सोच लिया यही नही रुखना हे खुद की भी किताब प्रकाशित करवाना हे।इस सपने को लिए इनका प्रयास प्रगति पर हे। इन्हें दर्द भरी,प्यार भरी,प्रोत्साहित करने वाली तमाम प्रकार की कहानियां एवं कविताएं लिखने का शौक है। यह बचपन से ही लेखन प्रतियोगिताओ में अव्वल दर्जे के लेखन रह चुके है।

लड़के गलत नही होते है

मैने चाहतो की सब मुरीदे तोड़ दी,
लड़का हु खुश हूँ,सब उमीदे छोड़ दी।
माता-पिता की छत्र-छाया में रहता हूँ,
ओरो के माता-पिता का भी में मान रखता हूँ।
मैंने चाहतों की सब मुरीदें छोड़ दी,
लड़का हूँ अपनी सारी ख्वाहिसे छोड़ दी।
खुश रहने लगा हूँ जबसे उम्मीदें छोड़ दी,
सब की इज्जत करता हूँ लड़का गलत नही हूँ।
घर में मेरी बहन का लाडला हु लेकिन बाहर भी मशहूर हूँ,
क्योकि में सब की बहन का भी एक सच्चा भाई हूँ।
हा में लड़का हूँ कभी न में रुखा हूँ,
लड़का हूँ इसलिए सरहद पर न में झुका हूँ।
लड़के घर से बाहर मम्मी पापा के बैगर होते है,
यदि लड़की घर की लक्ष्मी तो लड़के भी कुबेर होते है।
अपनों के सपनों के खातिर ये भी मजबूर होते है,
लड़के भी रोते है जब घर से दूर होते है,
लड़के भी गलत नही होते है।

लड़के गलत नही होते हे

क्या खूब लिखता हूँ,
घर की लड़की का हे मान
माना क़यामत के हर तजुर्बे पर लड़की हे अभिमान
घर की प्यारी राजदुलारी नही जाती शमशान
लड़का दिखलाता हे पंचतत्व का सम्मान
फिर क्यूँ सबने एक शख्सियत को अनदेखा किया..!

हम लड़को को,
आज हर कोई क्यों अनदेखा कर रहा
अगर लड़की धरती का आधार है तो
लड़के उस आधार की नींव होते है..!

जिंदगी लड़को को,
पर ज़िंदगी की कुछ पहेलियाँ है
वैसे लड़के अपने आप में एक संपूर्ण किताब है
कुछ मुश्किले लड़के को पत्थर बना देती है..!
परंतु हर जिम्मेदारी को बखूबी निभाता लड़का।

Deepjyoti Chowdhury

Deepjyoti Chowdhury embraces reading and writing as her escape from the real world as well as a window to it. She is a strong believer of Christ and Karma. Written in 100+ anthologies, she is the author of "Heartfelt musings" and "The staircase to freedom". Her main aim is to heal people and make them smile through her art of writing. You can follow her on Instagram at dj_writes_to_heal .

The Real Gems

When I often see my better half filled with burden,
My way of seeing things broadly widens.
The pressure that the males of the society face,
And have to run the unending competitive race.
From family to spouse, all depend on them;
They're the real warrior and precious gems.
Suffering all hardships all alone,
Firmly standing to be a family backbone.
Being constantly burdened with a stone,
Always ready for the challenges unknown.
We need to acknowledge that they're not always wrong,
Even in the most hurtful situation, they stand strong.
Just because of one, do not blame them all;
They will remain gems whether you accept or troll.

Deepanshu Singhal

Deepanshu Singhal, studied from commerce side and passionate for writeups and anthology. He is from Uttarakhand. He loves to write. He has many dreams which he wants to achieve and be standup poet once.

हमे भी दर्द होता है

रोते हम भी है चोट लगने पर
लेकिन किसी को बता नही पाते
सपने तो हमारे भी है
लेकिन घर की ख्वाइशो के आगे पूरे नही कर पाते
लगा देता है कोई जब झूठे आरोप हमपर
तब मुहँ पर कालियत और सिर पे जुतो का अम्बर होता है
मर्द को पत्थर का मत समझो जनाब
हमे भी दर्द होता है

हमेशा हम गलत नही होते
कभी कभी तुमसे भी गलती हो जाती होगी
इंसान ही तो है भगवान थोड़े ही
हमको भी तो तुम्हारी कुछ बाते बुरी लग जाती होगी
कभी हम ज़िन्दगी के गम भूलाने को एक दो पेग लगाले तो हमे शराबी
बता दिया जाता है
हुम इतने बुरे भी नही होते जितना हमे बना दिता जाता है

सीने मे दूनिया भर के गम छुपाए बैठे है
परिवार के लिए अपने सपने कुर्बान किए बैठे है
टूट जाते है हम भी सबको संभालते संभालते
ना जाने फ़िर भी क्यू हम "All Men are Dogs" का शीर्शक लिए बैठे है

Gaurangi Singh

Hope within eyes and sky as a limit, with a mixture of bubbly and bold character figuring and exploring ways to hone herself the future HR   department head, Gaurangi Singh. Pursuing Bcom from esteemed Delhi University for whom writing is what that keeps her sane! Strongly having a belief "Treat the people the way u want to be treated" Having a zest to live the life to the fullest! Writing has always been a way to express herself when she has no words! In this chaotic and deceptive world where nothing is true and everything comes for a price, writing is what that assures her that still, she can hope for Rainbows in dark valleys!!

<u>Is it so bad to me !!</u>

Am I being fragile when I let out what I have !!
Am I being stupid if I cry for someone who I love,
Is it bad to be just "myself"
For I also feel the pain when I get hurt,
For I also want to be flooded by cuddles from whom I love,
For I also want to be pampered like a baby.
With every drop of tear that I let out,
Doesn't prove that I am weak.
I have also swallowed the darkest secret of me,
I have also walked on the bed of thorns,
So, to see my loved one's who they want to be.
For I have also engrossed the emotional chaos of everyone
that has wept in front
Of me.
Taking all this burden that I hoist,
If my feet tremble and I fall down,
And look for a brace of love,
Is it so bad to me!
For I wanna say that " That nothing goes like what I think "
For this society has patriarchal notions that
Say's all for me.
That you are too stupid to be sad that so
So worthless and pointless,
For you are way stronger than this,
As men don't cry they say as
Their manliness decreases.
Before a Man, I am still a " Human Being"
Is it so strenuous to see???
For everyone say that all is going to be

Sheer,
For no one see's the dilemma that I bear!

Hansika SR

Hansika SR is a Chartered Accountancy student and a Carnatic singer by profession and a passionate writer, poet, a rhetoric public speaker and an enthusiastic learner of Vedic scriptures. She has brought numerous laurels through her versatility and her linguistic skills.

Men suffer too!

Where do men suffer, an instance!
Never am I the prey of this quintessence.

He makes everyone happy right when taking birth.
Brought out as family's protection with all mirth.
Grew up taking the responsibility of the family,
Still be the contemplated creator of the socialist anomaly.

He gets along being casual, though considered delusional
Always a matter of apprehension to women, well that's
usual.
Blooms to be a man of virtues and integrity.
A self-mastered guy, slips out to enamor a girl of
incompatibility.

Strives to sustain the relation despite the disregard
Though is unworthy here of being barred.
Letting her ruin his peace out, put to endure
Exhausted deadly with no heart's cure!

Not always do men create harm, they are harmed too.
They dolor their life till they find a true-blue.
They again magically fill colors to the new,
Giving sunshine, gets back the intense hue.

Men are not always right, neither wrong.
Yet not everyone accepts and takes them along,
Me a girl, never a feminist, nor of a machismo's ally,
Just showering my humane to the civil flunkey!

Harshavardini. M

Harshavardini. M from Coimbatore. She completed her schooling in National Model. She completed her BA. English Literature. She is also a co-author. She is passionate in her dance. Good qualities and kindness filled in her and hobbies are drawing, writing poems and doing embroidery designs. She spreads positivity and happiness around her.

<u>Why should boys have all the pain?</u>

Beautiful creature from god!
Who smiles in trouble and gathers his strength
One who never think for himself
It pain and pain but never felt down
His soul fills with pain but he tackle on and on
Love floats uninterrupted to mom and wife
The one soul see his wife as mom and
Immense sorrow break up once more he jumped up
Real man be honest and no matter how he pains inside
Handsome gentlemen are respected forever
No teardrop found in his face ,his happy smile carries on…..

Ishani Durba Purkayastha

Ishani Durba Purkayastha loves to live in the present without any tension for future. She loves dancing and writing. She is a professional dance choreographer and writing gives her happiness. She is also a bronze medalist in national level art and craft competition.

Mard ko dard nahi hota?

"Mard ko dard nahi hota" - yehi to use sikhaya tha...
to kya hua, agar uske samne, uske baap ne, uske maa pe haat
uthaya tha.
"Mard ko dard nahi hota" - yehi to use sikhaya tha...
To kya hua agar dahej ke liye uske behen ko zinda jalaya tha.
"Mard ko, dard nahi hota" - yehi to use sikhaya tha...
Isi liye to, usne apni biwi par atyaachaar kiya tha.
"Mard ko dard nahi hota" - yehi to use sikhaya tha...
Uske jazbato ko suruse, tumhi ne to dabaya tha,
tumhi to ho, jisne use bereham banaya tha.
"Mard ko dard nahi hota" - yehi to use sikhaya tha.

No one will notice -

She said, "Don't shout at me, I don't like it."
"But I didn't" - he TRIED to justify.
She screamed saying, "Now you are calling me a liar too."
"I'm sorry." - he replied and....
This is not a new story
I heard them quarrel every other night.
This is not strange that he is a boy.
Yes, he is a boy
who is abused by his girlfriend.
Yes, he is a boy who is afraid of shouting,
but he is a boy
thus, nobody will ever know about his grief.
He is a boy,
so no one will ever notice his pain.

Jeevitha. S

She is a girl with stupendous writing skills. Her heart is a castle abound with unbreakable courage, being contained with enticing dreams. Penning is her way of spreading aesthetic vibes among her readers. Being a libertarian is her pride. She loves to be a unicorn amidst the flock of sheep's!

Let's consider and let's get considered

Not a feminist alone but I'm a human too, in this world of justifying women's struggles and hardships let's look onto Men's stressful life. If you denote that it is hard to look upon your family and get the house chores done, of course it is equally difficult to be the foundation of it. It's a routine without a break, it's agreed. Being inside four walls doing all households looking after the children and family members with love differs from a stressful life that you face on the outside world where you have to earn for the well-being of the family and to satisfy their day to day needs and to provide them what they loved to have , women do it with love but men whether they like it or not they join a job just for the wellbeing of their family , whether they love it or not they always have a smile on their face simply as an eccedentesiast , when women get satisfied by seeing their family happy because of her actions men get happiness by looking on the brighter faces that smile when their needs get satisfied . Let's not be selfish by considering only our sufferings. Even Men undergo such emotional conflicts, we pour out everything but they never , they always fake their smile to see their family happy . Let's consider men and let's be considered as feminine.

Him !

He was born with responsibilities,
He grew up respecting women,
He cared and protected his sister,
He respected and loved his mother,
He stood as a good friend,
He loved his wife by all his heart,
He became even more responsible when his daughter was born,
He forgot his own needs; his family became his everything.
Why him always! Life indeed placed so many challenges on him.
People might have failed giving a try on his shoes,
He never complained he accepted everything and have been a genuine man.
Every man deserves this due respect, you are sometimes being unappreciated
But, you are always the one who sacrificed a lot .

J.Josephine Jesika

J.Josephine Jesika is from Sivanganga, Tamil Nadu. She is chasing her degree in English Literature. She loves to write and explore the unseen world through her words. She is a co-author of other two anthologies.

Not all are the same.

Not all the boys latch the door
To abuse an immature child.
Not all the boys shut his mouth
To speak out against the act of wild.
Not all the boys have a stony wicked heart,
Rather I would say by mind and heart they are even so smart.
Not all the boys are born to roam as a rogue,
In fact, there are some, who really care for their folk.
Not all the boys gaze a girl with an eye filled with lust,
Really, I would say there are some who stand as a true
symbol of trust.
Not all the boys leave their elders as orphans,
Indeed, there are many who worship their parents that are
concealed so often.
Not all the boys stand against the women rule,
Admittedly they are the only uplifting tool.
Not all boys seal the path of the girl's desire,
Truly I would say they never fell for girl's attire.
Not all the boys are meant to do wrong
Lively there are many who leads a family so strong.

Jyoti Matania

Born and brought up in Odisha, Jyoti is currently pursuing her bachelor's degree in political science. A girl who wants to chase her dream and writing has allowed her to connect with herself and people across the world.

You can connect her on her Insta handle theroyal_mataniagirl

Actually, why should boys

I heard it somewhere and it got stuck to me, "Feminism mean Men; men who have the courage to stand by the women in their lives and the women in society." Not all men have this but most of the men who have this we never talk or discuss them though. When a girl leaves her home after marriage, It's, a boy who holds her hand promising her to be there to influence the level of happiness, growth and success like no one else did. No one knows Varun Dahiya, husband of topper of civil services examination in 2017, Anu Kumari who had secured AIR 2. It was all possible because of the man who continuously encouraged her, pushed her, shored up for her by being her pillar of strength making her create her own identity. This is the real meaning of masculinity, unlike society who defines manhood is measured in strength, where there is no way to be vulnerable without being emasculated, where manliness is about having power over others. A boy is being responsible to join his father's business, to earn money for his family, to take his family ahead but somewhere that boy who wanted to fulfill his dream by being a cricketer, actor, chef and many more is still left behind. The boy who just wanted to be himself.... to live for his dreams is often blamed by the society. A man also has emotions, but we will probably never understand but we can see at least one pattern and that pattern is glaringly obvious. It's boys and boys are not always wrong.

Madhu Singh

Her name is Madhu Singh, she love to write motivational, and emotional quotes. She started writing in March 2020 and very soon she became a part of flairs and glairs as a co-author in the face of flairs and glairs she get a bit success in lit age.

She is hard-working and determined girl who never give up in any situation and she also make others motivate. She is a simple girl who love to talk and help and care about others.

Most of the people called her an innocent girl.

She love to enjoy and captured each and every moment of her life.

Boys life

Boys don't show off,
they hide their pain inside their heart.
They hide their feelings and emotions in their heart.
They don't cry front of people, but they cried inside in their
heart.
They know what is wrong and what is right.
That's why they always look bright.
They know the pain of their family that's why they work till
the night for give them comfortable life.
"Girls think that only they have emotions, but have a girl
ever asked to the boy that does he has emotions or not?
Is he not a person? He has emotions, he has feelings, he has
pain, but he never show-off, because he thinks about his
family that if I give-up then who will become recourse of my
family I need to be honest front of my family and others,
because if I will be strong then my family will be strong too.
So that's the boy's life.
"Boys don't show off".

Mansha Poddar

Mansha Poddar was born on 14th August 2003 in Sambalpur, Odisha. Since childhood her parents and teachers supported her in her writing skills. She is a sprouting bud of fantasy who loves to dress up her words. She aspires to become a well-known writer as well as a Forest Officer. She is a spiritual person and a devotee of God despite of any religion. You can reach her for more of her scribbled writings on Instagram at @perpetual_covet

.**Why always he?**

He has been brought up in households,
Which make up preach such false scrolls,
They tell him he will soon be the man of the house,
While he is just nine years old sitting in his couch,
It's not their fault you see,
This is what they've been taught since centuries,
That men don't feel and men don't cry,
Man up they told him, young boy, don't dare to be shy,
And as a kid, he once cried in public and people laughed,
As if they loved it and made his emotions half,
Then the kid wiped his eyes,
His smiling face was filled with lies.

Running out of pillows!

He wishes to talk to you about his journey,
But he does not know where to begin,
He is a product of failed social system,
Where expressing himself is consider as sin,
Look at his tears trip from his silence,
You need to talk to him and break this silence, So go.
Talk to your dad... ask him what his dreams were,
And what he really want to pursue,
Talk to your elder brother... ask him what he is going through,
And how he landed in this job he never wanted to,
Talk to your son... who might be really young,
But tell him that he needs to speak up,
And crying in public will never mean that he is weak,
But he can't cry himself every night as the world is running out of dry pillows,
Tell all of them that there is you to listen to them and take care,
Most importantly talk to yourself, look in the mirror and smile.

Meghana Dumpala

Her name is Meghana Dumpala, pursuing her dental UG course, passionate about writing. She feels writings can reach to people when they are written from heart. Apart from writing she love singing, dancing, cooking and travelling.

Treat him like human, before treating him as a man

"When he becomes a man, he is going to bring name and fame to our family"
"He is going to be the milestone of our family."
"He is going to earn more than I earn."
"He will fulfill my dreams which are left incomplete."
these are the things we here from the parents the moment he was born.

From the time he was bought into this world, he was expected to be the best out of all out there. He was expected to fulfill all the dreams which were left incomplete by his parents. He has just been expected from the moment he was born.

In most of the families…. sorry my bad, in all families, boys are meant to take the responsibility, he is expected to get the best job, he always gets compared to his friends saying, " he scored the highest marks, what are you doing? You always stick around him, what have you learnt from him?", compared with his cousins claiming, "he has settled so fast at early age, what are you doing, get a job… best job than others."
I wonder have they ever tried to know what he is interested at, or what field do he want to grow in?

And when it comes to society's point of view, "boys don't get hurt, no matter what we say or do." Seriously, are you even using your brains to claim such things against them.
He is a human before being a boy, at least try to recognize that for God's sake. Even he have feelings, even he cries, even he

gets hurt. If any boy cries, everyone states that he is sensitive, he is not manly, what by not crying, he proves that he is manly…. Are you crazy!!! And if someone is weak not as strong as others, they bully him being taunted with idiotic nicknames….and he will be compared to a girl.

Guys, everyone of us have feelings, boys are allowed to cry, it's not a crime to show their feelings, it's not any disorder to be weak, if he have different dreams apart from getting a job then it's not that your son is a failure, he is just going in a different direction from others. If everyone are aimed to become Mukesh Ambani, who will become Sachin, who will become Arjit Singh, who will become Bhagat Singh, it's okay to be different and have different ideologies to achieve in life.

Stop burdening them with your incomplete dreams, stop criticizing them for their in-capabilities, stop bullying them for showing their feelings…. Stop expecting from them more than you need to.

Expect for love, care, friendship, loyalty, honesty, but not these silly things. Treat them as humans before treating them as boy.

Meghna Chatterjee

She lives in passion and thrives in compassion.
Being a deeply emotional soul, she finds solace in writing poetries and stories.

He freed himself into Infinity

He freed himself into infinity
He was sitting in despair, he was crying in pain
He tried to explain is stand but all went in vain
He loved her with his heart and soul
Committed to his wow, truthful to his conscience, he never played the foul
But it was just his dearth of fame and money,
That made her soul grow dispassionate and tainted her depths with severe agony.
It was on that melancholic valentine's night
The invisible list of her expensive demands added to his plight.
Huddling through his purse for penny he failed to satiate her desires exorbitant and high
His soulful love got a severe blow and his genuine spirits an exhausting sigh.
She left the pristine purity of his gentle touch and compassion
Instead a purse heavy with pennies became her sole attraction
Blinded in grief and engulfed in pain he strangled his frustration into the harrowing clutches of that rope
From the dungeons of hypocrisy and drudgery he freed himself into an eternal slumber into the infinity of hope.

Muskan Sachdeva

Muskan Sachdeva hails from Basti, Uttar Pradesh. She completed studies from St. Basil's and is pursuing Chartered accountant along with B.com from Allahabad university. Writing was just a time pass earlier but then it became her passion. She has been co-authored in 10+ anthologies.

Not only girls suffer, Boys also do

A boy is not always wrong
Let us know the reason why he is so
May be his family expects a lot from him
Maybe he has family with no earning member
Maybe he had a heartbreak
Maybe he has been assaulted.

Not only girls, boys are also assaulted
They are tortured for many reasons
They are being abused too
They suffer depression too
They fear from gathering too
All they need is someone to listen.

Not only girls, boys also suffer from heartbreak
They also feel pain of losing their love
They also cry
They also want love
They also want someone who can hear them
They also want someone who can help them move on

Not always boys are wrong
Not always what a girl says is correct
Not always boys ill-treat girls
Sometimes what girl says is may be wrong said to take
revenge
Sometimes girls ill-treat boys to their works
Not only girls suffer BOYS ALSO DO.

Nanci Kabra

Nanci Kabra, a girl with many incomplete dreams. She is graduate this year in technology with future in technology

She belongs to kapasan (Chittor district) Rajasthan

And her heart devoted to nation her dream is to do something for the nation.

She loves writing poetry, prose, fictional story and also expresses her own feelings

She wrote before in four anthologies and also working for her solo she is very dedicated in writing, her only ambition to make her parents and nation proud

Check her on Instagram @mashupofthoughts(#mashupofthoughtss)

गलत नहीं तेरा लड़का हो ना।

तनहाई में तेरा आंसू बहाना
अपने जज्बातों का बिछाना
कभी-कभी थक के बैठ जाना
हारना फिर गिर के खड़े होना
गलत नहीं तेरा लड़का होना।

मां की गोद में सर रख के सोना
प्यार की याद में रोना
भगवान की पूजा करना
तुझे कोई संभाले इसकी मांग उठाना
गलत नहीं तेरा लड़का होना।

कभी-कभी सिर्फ खुद की सोचना
कभी जिम्मेदारियों से ऊपर उठकर खुद को देखना
कभी टूट ना तो कभी बिखर जाना
अपनी कमजोरी दिखाना
गलत नहीं तेरा लड़का हो ना।

<u>Why should boys</u>

Why should boys
always have to pay the bills
And not allowed to be ill
Always make to have the right decisions
And Not approved to weaken
They need you in the end
When they are completely broken

Why should boys
Are always have to take responsibility
Not to behave as a childish
Have to smile day and twilight
But never have to fall tears in grief

Why should boys
Have to be stronger and tougher
Are allowed to fall apart?
They also need support
When they are escort

Flairs and Glairs (Publication House)

Nithya Kanagaraj

Hi all. She's Nithya, currently pursuing BE ECE at Kongu Engineering College, Tamil Nadu. She loves to express her thoughts in a poetic perspective. Because she believes it opens a path to communicate with universe. She's a short story writer, blogger and artist too. Taste the happiness in your own way and live every moment.

Dive in my poetries at Instagram @the_poetic_quill_

Why?

Society's taboo tangled him
into abstract dreams.
There exists a self-war
Putting him into
Oratorical bruises.
"Can't I have my own rights?", the cells asked.
"You cannot cry. You're a man. Remember!",
the harsh voices warned.
With every disgust thrown,
Those uncontrolled drops
Suppressed unwillingly shouted,
"BUT WHY?"
Every saying crushed his
independence and chained
with an ever-lasting
Unwritten rule.

Request

Nature is a splendid algorithm that the mortal bodies can't figure out. There are many more mysteries till left hidden. One among those is the mankind. The truth is that we haven't learnt the whole about ourselves.

Beyond the human-made laws, the little fluttering souls in every one of us has a right to live in its own way. If the wish of souls doesn't affect any innocent lives, then there's no law for any of the mortal fleshes to pause them.

In that level, there won't be any gender specific. Equality should dominate.

A naive soul asked, "Hey Universe. Am I not allowed to express my feelings? Is there any curse of being in a man's body? Why does every little thing matter more than true expressions? Answer me!"

This society has no answer to this secretly weeping soul. They in fact jailed their feelings which is certainly a crime that the nature won't allow.

Feelings aren't meant for femineity alone. But for each and every single life in this space.

Pinki Bansal

Pinki Bansal, 19 years old, whatever i write its poem or shayaris doesn't show any kind of my reality. I am just fond of writing. Another, I am very happiest person in my life...

घर का बेट

रो रो रूठ गए आँसू मेरे,
पर माँ के सामने हँसना जानता हूँ
घर में खाना जिस दिन कम बनें
मैं 'भूख नहीं हैं माँ'कह कर टालना जानता हूँ
मैं एक बेटा हूँ...
बिन आँसू रोना जानता हूँ...
सपने तो बहुत कुछ हैं मेरे
पर पापा जो चाहे, मैं वो चाहता हूँ
कुछ ख़ुद के सपनें अधूरे,
कुछ पापा के सपनें मुकम्मल चाहता हूँ
पापा से जब मस्ती में कोई शर्तें लगे,
तो मैं जीत कर भी हारना जानता हूँ
मैं एक बेटा हूँ...
अपने सपनें ख़ुद तक रखना जानता हूँ...
बाहर की दुनिया देख,
मैं भी खुले आसमां, उड़ना चाहता हूँ
पर मेरी बहन के पर कटे हुए हैं
तो मैं कैसे आसमां छू सकता हूँ
ज़ख्म ज़ाहिर नहीं करती मेरी बहन,
पर यकीन मैं उसके सारे ज़ख्म जानता हूँ
मैं एक भाई हूँ...
अपनी बहन के दर्द जानता हूँ...
घर का बेटा हूँ मैं....
घर की जिम्मेदारी उठाना जानता हूँ...
घर का बेटा

Prachi shah

She is Prachi shah from Jharsuguda a small city in Odisha. Pursuing course of Chartered Accountant.

<u>Har ladka ek jaisa nahi hota</u>

Balatkar kuch ladke karte hain,
Badnaam sab ho jaate hain,
Zimmedariyo ke uljhan mein na jaane,
Kahan kab hasna bhul jaate hain.

Jab ishq use kuch bewaqt hota hai,
Sapne wo bhi apne sanjo leta hain ,
Lekin jab uska pyaara sapna chaknachor hota hai,
Aur ankho ke samne se koi apna gujarta hai,
Sach maano yaaro,mard ko bhi dard hota hai.

Pyaaj katne se uske bhi aashu aate hain,
Darpok karar kardiye jaate hai,
Agar andhero se lagta hai unhe dar,
Paalne ko wo apno ka pet,
Har shauk wo dafan kar jaate hain,
Ladko mai machiney kyu dhundte hai,
Aur rone pe kyu kehte hain, kya ladki ki tarah rota hai.

Ladke ro nhi sakte aisa kon kehta hai,
Humiliation,bullying unhe bhi bardast nhi hota hain,
maa ka aanchal, papa ka sahaara use hai jrurt,
Wo ladki hai uske saare ilzaam sahi hai,
Aisa zaroori hai kya harwaqt .

Priyanka Varma

Her name is Priyanka Varma, student of Masters of Pharmacy from Visakhapatnam.

She wants to convey everyone that "stop being afraid of what can go wrong and start being positive about what can go right".

<u>**Boys Don't Cry**</u>

It's very common to hear everyone saying "Hey stop crying.
Boys don't cry".
This is absolute non-sense.
We are teaching them that it's not okay for boys to feel pain
or sadness.
We are teaching them that there should be no space for
weakness and sensitivity in their hearts, and in order to be a
real man, emotions should be disregarded.
And then they grow up to become indifferent, cold and hard.
We made them inhumane, they forget how it is to feel.
So, let's cut the crap,
BOYS- you don't always have to be strong.!!
Sometimes asking for help is the bravest move you can
make; you don't have to go it alone...!!
It's ok to cry….!!
It's ok to show more than your anger….!!
It's ok to feel….!!
Don't keep all your feelings wrapped-up inside you,
Express yourself, don't ever let life shut you up...!!
You're a human, Express yourself…!!

They Too Deserve Respect

Not all boys are same, there are some boys who are different
There are some boys who know how to respect girls
Not every boy wants your body, not every boy questions
your character
Not every boy kindle in hunger's flame and not craves for
other's property to claim.
Not every boy's feature is doing weird gestures, some lads
are heroes with respected beard.
Not every boy desire to play with girls, some boys wants to
enter girls life via becoming ken doll – Barbie
Not every boy is a player of cheap games, some boys defend,
respect girls via their soul
Not every boy is bad boy, and being a boy is not that easy.
There are boys who may cheat and also there are boys who
live to see a smile in his girl's face.
Experiencedly saying,
ALL BOYS ARE NOT SAME, LET'S TREAT THEM
WITH THE RESPECT THEY DESERVE

Priyanshu Somkuwar

Here is Priyanshu Somkuwar from Nagpur, he is currently perceiving his graduation in Electrical engineering and started holding pen since from his first year. He has been a part of 5+ anthologies as a Co-author. His ambition is to become an IES Officer. He is passionate about writing and expressing his feelings into words.

Ladke ki juban-e-dastan

Jimmedariyon se bhari hai uski
Zindagi har pal use ehsas dilati
hai ki tujhe inn sabse ladna hai,
sangharsh Kar jeevan main aage
badhna hai.

Koshish karta hai wo ki sabko khush
rakh paye, dosto ke dard bhare kisase
khud hi aasani se suljha paye,
Kya Kare phir bhi ye duniya kosti hai use ye kahke,
ki saare ladke hote hi hai ek jaise...

Na chahte hue bhi wo ghar ke kamo
me hath batata hai,
phir bhi maa kahti hai ki mera beta
kisi Kam mein nahi aata hai.

Kya hua ladke hai to hame dard nahi
hota hai,
aakhir hame bhi shikayte karne ka
mauka chahiye hota hai.

Rahul Raj Srivastava

Rahul, he's a person who writes poems and raps, he acts and love to out of the box stuff. Always up for challenge, he always takes part in open mics.

Why we should always suffer?

Why should we always suffer?
We're not always wrong.
But aapko to accuse karna hai,
Even if your accusations are wrong.
Hamme bhi emotions hai,
Hame bhi rona aata hai.
Itne bhi hard nahi,
Bura sunte sunte, dhairya hi toot jata hai.
Par hamare aansu to kisiko nahi dikhte,
Aur stars,
Wo bhi to aaj to sirf macho hi bikte.
To expectations to honi hi hai.
Samaj se darkhwast,
Ye opinion kyu banayi tumne.
Kuchh bhi bura ho,
We're always framed!
Chahe galti ho na ho,
Jhoothi rape cases me jane kitne gaye jail!!
Kyu bhai?
Why we should always suffer?
We're not always wrong.

Rahul Sain

He is a young and dynamic person, With a broken heart and a fake smile.

मर्द का दर्द

मेरे जज्बातों को मजाक बताया गया
हर वक़्त मुझे सताया गया
जब उठाई हक में बात मेने
मर्द हूं बताकर चुप कराया गया,
औरत की वफा पर शक केसा
ये कहकर मुझे झूठलाया गया
मेरी दलीलों को फिजूल बताया
और जो निकले आंख से आंसू मेरे....
मर्द कभी रोते नहीं कहकर चुप कराया गया

अकेला

एक भीड़ है
पर तन्हा सा हूं...
मै कहीं ना कहीं बिछडा सा हूं
तू उठा कर सीने से लगा तो सही
मै अभी भी थोड़ा ज़िंदा सा हूं

R. Susanna Celsia

A passionate writer, published poet and blogger who aspires to impact lives through her writings

His diary

Today morning i got down in the town ,brother asked me to go to ,wearing a normal t shirt and jeans, I saw few girls in salwar and jasmine flowers on their head ,adorning their braids ,they had books in their hands ,mostly waiting for the bus to go to college .I did not know anything about the town, I look around couldn't find anyone else .I approached one of those girls ,and asked them, about the address ,brother had written in a small chit .Their reaction was surprisingly expected ,they rolled their eyes and almost cried afraid of me ? I understand all the brutality men have done, but does it mean that all of us are bad, I'm not saying trust every guy who asks you about address ,but the pathetic situation when I ask for help I have no one ,because I'm a man ??? If I stood their longer, I could be blamed of assault ,so I walked away saying thanks and walked figuring out the address as my heart burned and the broken pieces caused a fire with friction ,I was a faithful guy, I really loved her, I did not use her ,in her I saw the girl I would tie ,the sacred thread too ,in her I saw my wife ,my destiny but all she saw was my money ,time pass I really couldn't get back to normal after that, and now I'm going to another place to start fresh ,trying to get over mother's words I walk in agony ,all I here is you have to run a family ,you have to take care of your girl, I understand she will need space of bearing our child ,which I will share ,what is wrong in a girl sharing her husband's financial burden ,after all this the people of the town held my shirt and beat me up ,because I was a guy ,new face ,and all I'm tagged as a traitor because I am a male ??

Sahina Ghugha

Sahina from Jamnagar city of Gujarat is student of B.com at Saurashtra university. She is a poet and author. She is Co-author in 4 books and want to be amazing writer.

तो क्या हुआ अगर वो लड़का है?

तो क्या हुआ अगर वो लड़का है ?
दर्द में दिल उसका भी तो रोता है।
कौन कहेता है मर्द को दर्द नहीं होता ?
अंधेरों में रोने वाला एक मर्द ही तो होता है।

एक लड़के को समझ पाना इतना थोड़ी आसान है!
आकाश के तारों को गिनने के समान है।
तारे अनगिनत है, फिर भी टूटते रहेते है।
किसी की ख्वाहिश पूरी करने में जुटते रहेते है।

लड़का है वो, एक जीन्स में सालो गुजारता है।
बहन की शादी में आंसू नहीं, पसीना बहाता है।
राशन की बोरियां वो लड़का घर तक उठाता है।
रूठे हुए रिश्तेदारों को जी जान से मनाता है।

अपने परिवार को खुश देखना चाहता है।
फिर भी कभी उन्हीं के तानों को वो सहेता है।
जिम्मेदारियों का बोझ उस पर बढ़ता रहेता है।
फिर भी उसका दिल रोज़ लड़ता रहेता है।

Samikhya Swain (Ikhya)

Ikhya hails from silver city Cuttack. Currently, she is a student of class 12. She loves to write because it gives her relief. Not only a passionate writer but she also a painter, YouTuber and photographer. You can connect with her using her Instagram ID @triggered.ladki or simply drop a mail at samikhya123swain@gmail.com

<u>Boys don't cry</u>

From childhood,
I was taught boys cry,
I don't why?
Don't we have feelings,
Or it's only the role of girls to cry?
Don't we have emotions,
Or it's only the girls with have such affections?

I'm a boy,
From childhood,
I was taught boys don't cry,
I don't know why,
Can't we open our mouth,
To say even we face rape?

I'm a boy,
From childhood,
I was taught boys don't cry,
They are born to dominate,
I don't know why ?

Sapna Bhatt

Hey! It's Sapna, talking about writings then she is not a professional writer. She just love writing coz it makes her feel happy, it brings her peace...

ऐसा क्यों ...

दिल दुखी होने के बाद भी
उसे मुस्कुरा के सबसे मिलना पड़े... ऐसा क्यों
वो टूट चुका हो अंदर से पर
अपनों के ख़ातिर आगे बढ़ना पड़े... ऐसा क्यों
तुम दुखी हो तो रो रोकर आँसू बहा लो
पर वो एक आह तक भर ना सके... ऐसा क्यों
एक आँचल की चाह वो भी रखता है
एक साथी का साथ उसकी भी तमन्ना है
पर दिल में सौ दर्द छिपाये वो
किसी से कुछ कह भी ना सके... ऐसा क्यों
माना फूलों की चादर की उसे कोई चाहत नहीं
पर पैरों में काँटे लिए उसे
हर राह को पार करना पड़े... ऐसा क्यों !!!

Shikhar Pathak

Shikhar Pathak from Awadh, who in his life believes in spreading Kindness and Laughter in the city, has grown up being in close influence of Emotions and now pen both love and separation in his own unique way to leave his readers mesmerized and amazed.

साल भर

मैंने साल भर जाग कर रातें देखी, लोगों की मुस्कुराहटें देखीं, और रोते लड़के देखे, मैंने अपने परिवार को देखा और उनकी बेबसी देखी, मैंने बहन को देखा और उसके सपने देखे। मैंने मंदिर में मूर्ति के पीछे और तुलसी के गमले में देखा।

मैंने दादी कि आंखो में देखा, मैंने गुरुजी से पूछा और शराबी से भी। मै साल भर दीवार बना रहा। मुझे वो नहीं मिली।

लोगों को प्यार नहीं मिलता,इज्जत नहीं मिलती, दहेज़ और फरेब नहीं मिलता।

मुझे सब मिला बस वो नहीं मिली। किसी मंदिर में, सड़क पर, दवाइयों से आसमान के तारों में या मेरे दोस्त की बातों में, मुझे वो कभी नहीं मिली।

में अगले साल रात भर सोया, दिन भर पिया, दवाइयां,आंसू याद और धोखे।
मै साल भर के लिए भगवान हो गया।
वो मेरे सिरहाने बैठे मेरा सिर सहला रही थी।
जन्नत जमीन हो गई थी।
मैंने उसका हाथ पकड़ना चाहा,वो चली गई,
दवाइयां, आंसू सब बारिश बन गए मै कीचड़ हो गया।
मैं साल भर कीचड़ रहा, वो साल भर बारिश बन बरसी।
मैं जीवन भर कीचड़ रहूंगा, पर अब सूखा पड़ता है, कई सालों से बारिश नहीं हुई।
मैं सुखी मिट्टी हूं, जो जल्दी उद जाती है और आजकल हवा बहुत तेज हो गई है।

<u>Those Stains</u>

Trapped in the pages of time, a mildly withering lover, whose screams can never be blown out from the heart, he is always looking in a very distraught manner towards his lover while decorating the bundle of thoughts.

In dark as if out of the agony of depression, he flinches even when he says his agony.... People keep distance from me, they say What to write on someone's ruthlessness and stain? What will you gain from this?
Write on beauty, about someone who owns the lake of beauty. But had they ever thought of those who are holding those stains, who took the pain of that love... How the questioners here ended their beauty with such ease? ...
Will writing on them dry up their pens?

Every person sprinkles only his colored pen on the atomizer pages but I worship the black ink and write Those same stains.

Shivani Shrikant Sarwade

Shivani, a future pharmacist living in the city of God Vitthala-Pandharpur.

She is an ambitious girl who follows her heart and loves to write what her heart says!! Student of science but also admirer of arts too.

She can sense God in her parents along with that she believes in love, kindness and humanity too.

<u>**They aren't always wrong**</u>

Yes, why should boys??
They might have watery eyes.

Boys are not always wrong,
Even though they are so much strong.

They always care for everyone,
But expect the same from no one.

All they need is just trust and support,
They even know, who is perfect!

Boys crave for a little bit of respect & love,
It's the thing that they every time deserve!

Yeah, they need those helping hands while facing the
crushing defeats.
But sometimes they get only cheat.

They too dream to build a huge empire.
In their wings, just wait to bring a fire.

With lots of burning desires,
They walk for a mile bare...

Sheela Suman

शिला सुमन जी एक गृहणी है, उन्हें बचपन से लिखना ,पढ़ना, घूमना, बागवानी करना, लोगो से मिलना और बातें करना पसन्द रहा है। उन्हें अपने मन के भावों को शब्दों के रूप में ढालना अच्छा लगता है ।

सारा दर्द लड़के ही क्यों सहे ?

अचानक पत्नी के जोर-जोर से आवाज लगाने पर आकाश की नींद खुल गई।

खुद को पूरी तरह जागृत करने की कोशिश के बाद जब बात समझ आयी तो उसे यह समझने में देर न लगी कि कल बिजली बिल जमा न कर पाने के कारण आज श्रीमती जी की पसंदीदा टीवी सीरियल के समय ही बिजली विभाग ने उनके घर के कनेक्शन की पुंगी बजा दी है।

घर नजदीक होने के कारण लंच ब्रेक पर आकाश घर आकर खाना खाने के बाद कुछ मिनट की झपकी लेना पसंद करता था। पर आज के इस माहौल ने उसके खाने और आराम को हराम कर दिया।

 उसने कई बार पत्नी को कहा कि अगर समय मिले तो तुम भी कभी कभार इन कामों में मेरा हाथ बटा दोगी तो मेरी व्यस्थता थोड़ी कम हो जाएगी, क्योंकि मेरे पास भी इतने सारे काम होते हैं कि कभी कभी भूल जाता हूं कुछ कामों को।

ऑफिस के कामों में भी आज प्रतिस्पर्धा का माहौल है, तो वहां भी सौ प्रतिशत दिमाग को एकाग्रता चाहिए। सारे कामों को निपटाते हुए मुझे भी थोड़ी दिमागी सुकून की जरूरत होती है, तो कभी कभार ये छोटी-मोटी भूल हो जाती है।

पत्नी ने कहा, मैं यह सब काम नहीं कर सकती। यह आपकी जिम्मेदारी है।

इतना सुनने के बाद आकाश यह सोचने पर मजबूर हो गया कि क्या मैंने इतनी छोटी सी बात अगर पत्नी से चाही तो यह मेरी गलती थी ?

क्या यह सब मैंने सिर्फ अपने लिए किया था, तो फिर आज जो मैंने कोर्ट में किया क्या वह गलत था ?

क्योंकि आकाश एक ईमानदार और कर्तव्यनिष्ठ वकील होने के नाते अपने हर केस को सच्चाई की बुनियाद पर लड़ता था, यह बिना देखे कि उसका मुवक्किल औरत है या मर्द ।

आज फैमिली कोर्ट में इसी तरह के एक केस को हल करते उसने सोचा था, कि हम मर्द अपने परिवार के प्रति अपनी जिम्मेदारियों से उन्हें खुश कर पाने की काबिलियत रखते हैं।

पर इस घरेलू वाक्या ने उसके इस सोच पर प्रश्न चिन्ह लगा दिया, कि हम लड़के कितनी भी कोशिश कर ले पर वही हर जगह गलत क्यों साबित किए जाते हैं।
क्या किसी काम को भूल जाना किसी कारणवश उनके लिए जायज नहीं ?
फिर आज उसने एक निर्णय लिया कि अब सर से कुछ जिम्मेदारियों को उतारना जरुरी हो गया है, क्योंकि लड़के भी तो आखिर इंसान ही है तो फिर वह हर जगह गलत कैसे हो सकते है?

अगर हर जगह यह दावे किए जाते हैं कि मर्द और औरत गाड़ी के दो पहियों की तरह होते हैं तो फिर इस तरह की दोहरी मानसिकता क्यों?
क्यों नहीं लड़के अपने मन के भावों को रोकर चिल्लाकर या विद्रोह जताकर बता सकते हैं? किसने ऐसे नियम बनाए हैं कि मर्द एक फौलाद है, जिन्हें दर्द या तकलीफ नहीं होती?

यह सब सोचते सोचते आकाश कब कोर्ट रूम में जा पहुंचा, उसे पता ही नहीं चला पर एक नए नजरिए को साथ लिए, और इस सोच से उसे आत्मसंतुष्टि का एहसास हुआ। उसने खुद को बहुत हल्का महसूस किया अपने खुद के बनाये दाएरे से मुक्त होकर।

Shreya Gupta

She is a young poet. Writing is her passion, A strong believer in the power of positive thinking. Shreya Gupta, a graduate girl from Patna Women's College. She wants to serve the nation by fulfilling her future dream and ambition. She is fond of dancing.

Carries hope to learn off all the time. Blend of sensible and sometimes a funny form.

<u>कुछ अनकही बातें</u>

मर्द को दर्द नही होता,

ये बात कुछ हज़म नही होता,

जज़्बात छुपाते है वो,

इसका ये मतलब नही उन्हें कष्ट नही होता,

समाज ने शायद ये कायदा बना दिया है,

मर्द को समाज मे पत्थर का दर्जा दिया है,

वो रो नही सकते,

अपने जज़्बात बयां नही कर सकते,

दर्द उन्हें भी होता है जब चोट लगती है,

जब वक़्त रुलाती है,आँख उनकी भी भर आती है,

माँ के प्यार को ममता कहा गया,

पर कोई शब्द नही बना,

जो पापा के प्यार को बयां कर पाया,

जरुरी नही जो आँसु बहाये,

वो मर्द ना कहलाये,

दिल उनका भी दुखता है,

रातो मे अँधेरे से डर उन्हें भी लगता है,

सिसक-सिसक कर वो भी कई रात सोये है,

समाज के कुछ दरिंदो के कारण वो भी रोये है,

चीख को अपने दबाकर कर,परिवार के लिए जीते है वो,

क्यों नही कोई बताता उन्हें,की कितना गलत करते है वो,

दिल तो सबका एक है,तो क्यों पत्थर बना दिया जाता है उन्हें,

सौ बोझो से जिन्दगी मे क्यों दबा दिया जाता है उन्हें,

कोई तो उन्हें बताये,

मर्द वही है जो जज़्बातों के साथ,

समाज मे वो सदियों चले सोच को हटाए,
वो भी अपने जज़्बात दुनिया को बताए।।

Sonal Tripathi Mishra

Sonal Tripathi Mishra, an MBA graduate from a renowned institute, a recruitment professional. Writing since a very young age, an avid book reader, music lover, traveler and an ardent fan of art & aesthetics. Loves exploring & working on different attributes of human emotions through reading, writing and painting. Trying to create awareness n love for reading in young talents in today's technology driven society through her book reading classes n activity sessions. A well-grounded individual who lives with passion, dedication and grace.

tripathisonal12@gmail.com

Instagram- alfaaz_sonal

ये आम से लड़के

तमाम ज़िंदगी के पेच-ओ-खम से गुज़रते हैं
हर दर्द को सहते हैं,
फिर भी धीरे से मुस्कुरा लेते हैं
ये आम से लड़के

ज़िंदगी की तल्ख़ियों से रोज़
चार - ओ - नाचार होते हैं
थक कर भी ना रुक पाते हैं
ये आम से लड़के

अपनों की उम्मीदों को ज़हन में सहेजते हैं
ख़ुद की ख़्वाहिशों को
वापस जेब में रख लेते हैं
ये आम से लड़के

वक़्त की धूरी पर बस दौड़ते रहते हैं
समाज के पैमाने पर हर रोज़ ही तुलते हैं
फिर भी ना ठहरते हैं
ये आम से लड़के

दुनियादारी की जद्दोजहद में
पराये शहरों में भटकते हैं
नम आँखों को आहिस्ता से छुपा लेते हैं
ये आम से लड़के

एक तरफा सोच

महिलाओं के अधिकार और शोषण के बारे में तो कई ग्रंथ लिख डाले हैं, जो कि पूर्णतः ज़रूरी भी है लेकिन प्रकृति के दूसरे आयाम पुरुष को अनदेखा करना भी ग़लत है| ज़िंदगी की कशमकश में उलझते हैं कभी एक पिता बनकर, कभी पुत्र, कभी पति और कभी भाई| ज़िम्मेदारियों को अपने मज़बूत कन्धों पर मुस्कुराते हुए उठा लेने का सामर्थ्य, ईश्वर ने पुरुष को प्रदान किया है|

ये भी सत्य है कि कुछ पुरुषों के कर्मकांड की वजह से हम सभी को एक ही तराजू में तोल देते हैं| आज कल कितने ही प्रकरणों में , हम बिना सोचे, बिना सत्य की पहचान किये पुरुषों को कटघरे में खड़ा कर देते हैं| चाहें फिर वो दहेज का मामला हो, ऑफिस- कॉलेजों आदि में होने वाली छेड़छाड़ के किस्से; हमारा पलड़ा हमेशा औरतों की तरफ झुक जाता है| बिना पड़ताल किये ही हम पुरुष को दोषी मान लेते हैं, क्या ये सही है? ऐसी ही एकतरफा सोच के कारण कितने ही घर बिखर जाते हैं, निर्दोष और उनके घरवालों को जेल और तिरस्कार झेलना पड़ता है| जीत हमेशा सत्य की ही होनी चाहिये चाहें वो किसी भी और खड़ा हो|

अंत में बस इतना ही कहना चाहूँगी, किसी के भी बारे में राय बनाते हुए, हम आँखें और दिमाग खुले रखें और किसी के भी प्रति पक्षपाती सोच ना रखें| पुरुष और स्त्री प्रकृति का आधार हैं, एक के बिना दूसरा अधूरा ही रहेगा, इसलिए दोनों की ही भावनाओं को यथोचित् सम्मान देना चाहिए|

Subananthini. R

Subananthini. R is from Sivagangai, Tamil Nadu. She is pursuing her UG in PSG College of arts and science, Coimbatore. She is a budding writer who loves to explore the world in different perspectives. She is not a famous writer, yet she strives to be one. She is a co-author of two anthologies "SECLUDED HEARTS" and "UNSAID WORDS".

The Fair Mortal

He is someone who seems to be tough
But not really,
He tolerates one's nonsense,
But it doesn't mean he is out of sense
He never gives tips for servants,
But he donates to orphans in secret
He never treats people with parties,
But he always helps poor to make his heart ease
His casual look makes others unpleasant,
But he never does something aberrant
He sounds to be bothersome,
But his actions are always lovesome
He overlooks everyone in his family not because he is
doubtful,
But he is over-protective and wants to be careful
He scolds people, but he is not vicious
He is always as righteous as ever,
And as pure as fresh flower
He is someone who wishes to be independent,
But also he is someone I, you and anyone can depend.

Suhita S

Suhita, pursuing her MA in English Literature, a Charming girl, who loves the magical spark of life on holding the air of positivism, her love for crazy fantasies never ends, she acts to make the most of every second by loving the simplest form of each individuals. She had been Co-author of 20+ anthologies under various publication and many more in progress. She is also a book reviewer. Her poems are published in the Magazine 'Artistic Athena' of June and July edition and in Digital Magazine 'Shelves Of Arts and Literature' Volume-1. She observes and feels everything by heart, spreading her colors all over. Her thoughts were soulfully penned!
(Instagram Handle @sparkling_wink)
(Mail Id: suhichutty171@gmail.com)

<u>Being a male - Praise or Malediction ?</u>

Yeah! A baby boy!
"He is our family king"
"My heir, My soul, My proud"
"He is going to be Mom's son" favoritism
"Dress up like a prince - family prestige"
"Our Brave Warrior"
"Splendid by you, My son!"
"Hero for Girls"

Contrasting,

"No use of you born to me as a boy, better had none!"
"Shame of you without job?"
"Are you still fed by your mom?" Sarcastically
"Dress up like a gentleman – non-updated"
"Are you feared? Is that tears from your eyes?"
"Can't you manage by yourself?"
"Love sick? - a weak heart!"
"I see no characteristics of a male in you"

Dear Male mates,
You are not a toy to be emotionless
Fear and tear are common for human
You are doing your best to keep up responsibilities
Ups and downs may cross
But that doesn't question your manhood
I respect you in all ways
I tend to understand your feelings

As a daughter of father, Sister of brother, Wife of husband
You are not a cold-hearted stone
To be blamed and played.

Surbhi Bairagi

Surbhi lives in Indore. She is a published author. She loves to write on motivational, inspirational quotes and realities of life as well. She is calm, dedicated and industrious. Hope you like some of her write ups.

सिर्फ लड़के ही सारा दर्द क्यूँ सहे?

क्या हम अक्सर ये सोचते रहते है कि लड़को को किसी भी चिज़ का कोई असर नही होता?

क्या ज़्यादातर लड़कियां ये सोचती है , कि लड़को मे किसी भी प्रकार की कोई भावना निहित नही होती ?

तो बेशक़ आप गलत है । क्योंकि दिल लड़को मे भी होता है । ये सच है कि वो कभी अपनी अन्तरीय तक़लीफों भरी भावना को ज़ाहिर नही करते। बचपन से ही उनमे हर चिज़ को खुल के जीने का शौक होता है। वो अपने व्यंग्यात्मक रचनाओं से लोगो को हसाने मे ही अपना ज़्यादातर समय व्यतीत करते है। वे अकेले होने पर समस्याओं पे विचार ज़रुर करते है, पर कभी भी अपनी समस्याओं को ज़ाहिर नही करते और करते भी है तो केवल कुछ समय के लिये । जिसे वो बहुत ही होले होले सह लेते है।

पर उन्हे कभी कभी इतनी गहराई से समझा नही जाता । उन पर कई इल्जाम भी लगाए जाते है, किसी एक लड़के की गलत हरकतों की वजह से सारे लड़को को गलत साबित किया जाता है । परिवार मे किसी के जाने का दुख उन्हे भी होता है, किसी प्यार को खोने का दुख उन्हे भी बहुत गहरा होता है। दोस्तों से खफ़ा होने पर दर्द उन्हे भी होता है, पर वे अपने चेहरे पर ज़रा शिकन नही दिखने देते। हमारे पिता का अस्तित्व भी यही है । उनके हर ना के पीछे बहुत गम्भीर कारण छिपा होता है।और यही उनकी ताक़त और सबसे बड़ी काबिलियत का उदाहरण भी होता है। इसलिए उनके हर कदम पर साथ देना हमारा दायित्व होता है। उन्हे ही इस अनकहे दर्द से हमे उभारना है। ये वक़्त अब सिर्फ हाथ मिलाकर चलने का है।

V. Heymonth Kumar

This is Mr. V. Heymonth Kumar who writes poems in the pen-name, "Heymonth Ninja". He is an International Writer. He lives at a village of Erode, Tamil Nadu in India. His poetry, "Pandemic Curse", has published in Sydney, Australia. His research article, "An Echo of Ignored Screams", has published by Authors Press in Delhi. He wrote three books of short story in Tamil and published them through Notion Press in Chennai. He is a Shakespearean Theatre Artist who acts and directs Shakespeare's plays. He got various awards for his tremendous success in educating and enacting English literature.

<u>From a masculine heart</u>

Life is a race since the birth of a male,
Till his peaceful death, it is a painful tale;
Parents allow us to play any type of game,
When we get wounds, they treat us as shame;

Cute sisters do nothing for the boys,
And purposefully take away all of our toys:
People want to laugh by making us to cry,
They advise us, "You are a boy, do not be shy".

Emotions wave as ocean, but we hide all in a tumbler,
We do not want to be ridiculed by you with howler---
From adolescence, the world insists us to be brave,
Even a tempest comes in life, to our aged grave;

Being the breadwinner is not easy and fun,
We are always forced to work hardly and win!
Every "Women's day", we wish our sister,
Not even she respects us by calling as 'Mister'

In the masculine society, males are oppressed,
Count the suicide rate of who were depressed;
When a man gets married, he should work twice,
For earning every bowl of masala and rice;

All of the responsibilities fall on men's heart,
We are mastering the field of traumatic art---
Do you ever think, "Why men are tall?"
We are helping women by even our fall;

As little boys, we sacrifice our lovely things,
To our sisters, angels, who have hearty wings:
In our old age, we stay active with care,
And have our unfulfilled desires to share;

Do not consider men are ugly and waste,
We make the world to be beautiful with taste;
Men are the pillars for prospective women,
Who want to come out from the imprisoned den;

Oh, by Shakespeare's seven stages of life,
Men work for mother, sister, daughter and wife;
We never desire to dominate women in the society,
Please, do not blame and frame us to be guilty.

Yamini Sona Vaishnavi

Yamini Sona Vaishnavi is a budding writer who pursues her III UG of graduation in English Literature. She has a great love for writing and she believes that the only medium of emotions is words in the form of poems. She has a great passion of playing with words. She, being a budding writer, wishes to express her thoughts to the readers that pouring down our emotions in the papers can take her ideas to their hearts. She is already a co-author of two anthologies. She wishes to keep showering her writings with her very favorite weapon - the pen.

<u>Two - Faced ? Was it spotted ?</u>

He is the one who the mob expects for celebration of birth.
To make them smile, he comes out of the womb.
We think he smiles now at the moment.
But, was it spotted that his body was light and his shoulders heavy denoting his responsibilities every moment?

He is the one who the mob expects to be in gangs.
To make them smile, he goes out to adventure.
We think he smiles now at the moment.
But, was it spotted that his own residence became a grief for him and that's why he had to opt for outings?

He is the one who the mob expects to be obedient.
To make them smile, he changes his inside out completely .
We think he smiles now at the moment.
But, was it spotted that he cut his pretty little alluring wings on his own self just for the sake of others?

He is the one who the mob expects for wedding approaches.
To make them smile, he takes up the steps.
We think he smiles now at the moment.
But, was it spotted that he had some other dreams with someone else to lead a merry life?

He is the one who the mob expects for funeral of dead.
To make them feel satisfied, he takes up the charge.
We think he feels so strong at the moment.
But, was it spotted that he not only laid his beloved body in the coffin but also placed his heart along with it?

Why should pain travel only with boys?
Let the almighty drop them from pain's choice!

Yumkham Shelina Devi

Shelina has completed her Masters in Applied Genetics. Her passion of scribbling down her thoughts molded her to share her writings with people. She wanted to convey her thoughts and messages through her poems.

Told to be

He was told to be unafraid,
Reveal every deep layer tearing himself apart
He crawled beneath the thorns,
He bleeds but he was told not to shed tears;
It's the hormones, not his fault.
Buried his emotions with the veins,
He took an oath never to lose himself
Took every pain, hiding behind the smile
Sunny days are shivering,
Rainy days made his throat parched;
It's the seasons, not his fault.
Yes, he is the man.
No, he is not perfect.

Flairs & Glairs

Flairs and Glairs, a platform by a student for the students. We are esteemed youth struggling to carve out our path for our future and we follow a basic mindset Since everyone is not born with all-round skills. Joining hands with people who are born to execute it with perfection is the best way to evolve. Self-Evolution is the need of the hour but, evolving as a community is what we strive for. The initiative as kickstarted by, Founder- Mr. Shubham Shah with the motive to utilize the skillset and talent of writing has now a team of 10+ people who are actively participating into newer forms of learning and discovering talents among youngsters. We Provide platform and services like Publishing opportunities, Open mics, Workshops, Hands-on training. Operating with Brand Name Of Flairs and Glairs (Publication House), we offer the chance of elevating a passionate writer to an esteemed author With Brand name Teekhe Zasbaaat, We bring to you an opportunity to get accustomed with the Public Speaking and Presenting of Thoughts along with regular challenges to brush up your inking spirit. The newest initiative to extend our services we introduced in a new writing Platform- The Glittering Fables and Ink Over Tears.

We Choose to Fly Like A Falcon than to be a

Leg Pulling Crab.

To Know More: Infoline – 7781900870
Mail Us At-
flairsandglairs@gmail.com / info@flairsandglairs.in
Or Visit is at
www.flairsandglairs.com / www.flairsandglairs.in
Social Handles- @flairsandglairs @teekhezasbaaat